WELCOME TO

Beast Quest

D1464756

Collect the special coins in this book.
You will earn one gold coin for
every chapter you read.

1

Once you have finished all the chapters,
find out what to do with your gold coins at
the back of the book.

PiETRo

With special thanks to Tabitha Jones

For Louis Tejani, Dylan Tejani and Brian Dowling

www.beastquest.co.uk

ORCHARD BOOKS

First published in Great Britain in 2014 by The Watts Publishing Group
This edition published in 2018 by The Watts Publishing Group

1 3 5 7 9 10 8 6 4 2

Text © 2014 Beast Quest Limited.
Cover and inside illustrations by Steve Sims
© Beast Quest Limited 2014

Beast Quest is a registered trademark of Beast Quest Limited
Series created by Beast Quest Limited, London

A CIP catalogue record for this book is available from the British Library.

ISBN 978 1 40835 868 9

Printed and bound in Germany

The paper and board used in this book are made from wood from responsible sources

Orchard Books
An imprint of Hachette Children's Group
Part of The Watts Publishing Group Limited
Carmelite House, 50 Victoria Embankment, London EC4Y 0DZ

An Hachette UK Company
www.hachette.co.uk
www.hachettechildrens.co.uk

VISLAK
THE SLITHERING
SERPENT

BY ADAM BLADE

ORCHARD

CONTENTS

Dear reader,

Do not pity me – my spells may be useless now, but my sixth sense will never go. Evil is afoot in this once peaceful kingdom. Jezrin the Judge may have been defeated by brave Tom, but his minions do not rest. Our many Quests have taught me that an enemy beaten back will return stronger than before.

Tonight I had a vision of the pale moon turning black. What it means is not clear, but a new menace stalks the land of Rion, and I fear it will spread to Avantia. My wizard instincts tell me that our enemies plan to tip the balance of nature, turning Good to Evil. A hero will be needed to stand against the dark forces. Can you guess who that hero might be?

Aduro, former wizard to King Hugo

PROLOGUE

Ralph pulled his mule to a stop. He wiped the sweat from his face and squinted into the scorching wind. In front of him there was nothing but endless sand dunes baking under a blue sky. Ralph sighed and patted his mule's neck.

"Whatever happens now, Esther, you've done me proud," he said. The mule stood quiet, her skinny shoulders slumped. Ralph slid to the ground. His hands shook as he unscrewed his flask and tipped it up. A few warm drops fell onto his tongue, then nothing.

"If we don't find water soon," he muttered, "we'll both be as dead as this desert. City of Snakes? Thirty days we've been travelling, and nothing."

Ralph looked out across the desert. The colours seemed too bright. They pulsed and swam before his eyes. The wind howled like mocking laughter.

He pulled out a map and traced their path almost to the torn edge of the parchment, where there was a picture of a coiled snake.

The City of Snakes.

"Should be right about here,"
Ralph said. "So where's my treasure?"
Gold, maybe... Jewels. His pulse
quickened at the thought. But when
he swallowed, his throat felt as dry
as dust.

A hot gust of wind ruffled Ralph's
map. He looked up. A twisting eddy
of sand was sweeping towards him.
Not another dust devil! Esther rolled
her eyes, her hooves scuffing the dirt.

"Oh, no, you don't!" Ralph cried.
But the animal's reins slipped
through his fingers as she lolloped
down the dune.

"Get back here!" Ralph shouted,
lurching after her. The sand shifted and
he put out his staff to steady himself,
but he lost his footing and fell.

"Ahhh!"

He landed on his back and lay still.

A high wall, the same deep red as the desert, rose above him. Two thick posts framed an opening in the wall.

Ralph snatched up his staff, making for the doorway. The posts were carved with swirling lines. Ralph ran his fingers over them and grinned. *Snakes!*

Inside, crumbling sandstone buildings lined a deserted, sandy street. The sand ahead started to boil and rise. It fell in crimson sheets from a towering, dark red form. Ralph trembled in horror as a long, muscled body rose up before him. *A snake? But it's the size of a tree!*

The creature turned its broad, flat

head slowly towards him showing
blazing yellow-orange eyes. A black
tongue flitted from between its razor-
sharp fangs. Ralph watched, frozen
with terror, as the snake's huge mouth
stretched open, wider and wider.

Thick, dark liquid spurted from its jaws. *Venom!* Ralph threw his hands up to protect his face.

The liquid hit him like a blow. A great weight of thick, sticky fluid poured down his arms and over his face. It burned his eyes. He couldn't see! He tried to wipe the venom away, but his elbows wouldn't bend. The venom was hardening! He could feel it creeping down his back and over his legs. He fell to his knees under the weight of the goo. His arms and legs were stuck fast. He could feel his blood pounding as the liquid blocked his nose. Soon, he wouldn't be able to breathe...

The last thing he heard was the joyful hiss of the snake...

1

OUT OF TIME

The wind buffeted Tom as he climbed
down the mountain. It tugged at his
hair and clothes and snatched the
breath from his throat. He reached for
another foothold, and eased himself
downwards. He had climbed up the
peak to release Raffkor the bull-Beast
from Kensa's Evil enchantment. Now
that Raffkor was free, the next part of
Tom's Quest awaited him.

Tom craned his neck to look down. Elenna was climbing down too, just above him, and below stood Silver, her wolf, and Storm, Tom's stallion.

When he reached the bottom, he shook out his aching arms.

Storm trotted to his side and Silver pressed his warm nose into Tom's palm. Tom smiled and stroked the animals' coats.

"I'm so glad that Raffkor is free from Kensa's enchantment," Tom said to Elenna. "I had to cut off his black horn to do it. But another grew back."

"And you found the starleaf for Vedra's cure," Elenna said, grinning.

Tom flipped open his leather satchel. The small five-pointed plant inside looked as fresh as when he had picked it at the top of the peak.

Elenna squared her shoulders. "Now we just need three more ingredients to make the elixir to save Vedra," she said.

"Let's hope we can get them in time," Tom said. He looked up.

The moon was a white crescent against the pale blue sky. Tom frowned. It was growing by the day. They had to be back in Avantia's capital city before the full moon, with all four ingredients. If they failed, there would be no cure for Vedra the Green Dragon, suffering under Kensa's spell. Without a cure, the Good Beast would be lost to the witch's Evil for ever.

Elenna's hand fell on his shoulder. "We'll do it," she said.

Tom nodded. "We have to. But the ingredients are scattered to the corners of the kingdom and guarded by Kensa's enchanted Beasts. We don't have a moment to lose."

"Tom! Elenna!" Tom turned to see Wilfred the Beast Keeper trotting towards them on Breeze, Arcta's golden-brown feather bobbing in his hand.

"You're back!" Wilfred cried. "I knew you'd do it." He held Arcta's feather out to Tom. "You'd better take this back. I've had enough adventures to last me a lifetime!"

Elenna smiled. "We couldn't have saved Raffkor without you," she said, "but you should get back to the palace and give King Hugo the news."

Tom nodded. He pointed towards a winding path that disappeared over the horizon. "If you follow that road," he said, "it will take you home. But it will be many days' travel."

"I'll take Wilfred to the palace," a cheerful voice said from behind them. Tom turned to see Daltec's smiling face.

"Daltec!" Wilfred started towards the young Wizard. "How is Vedra?"

Daltec's smile faded. He looked down at the dusty ground. When he raised his eyes, they were grave. "More and more of his scales have turned black," he said. "It is as

Aduro feared. By the next full moon, Kensa's lunar blood potion will have taken hold. Vedra will be lost to Evil for ever."

Wilfred swallowed. "Please send me to him, Daltec," he said. "I should be at his side."

Daltec nodded, then clicked his fingers. Wilfred vanished.

"We must leave too," Tom said. He reached into Storm's saddlebag and pulled out his magic map. Near the bottom, a deep red glow pulsed steadily. A word appeared in curly writing. *VISLAK*.

Tom nodded slowly. He had met Vislak once before. He was a mighty Beast, a great red snake as tall and thick as an oak tree. Now Vislak was cursed, he would be a fearsome enemy. Tom turned the map towards Daltec and Elenna.

"Look," Tom said, pointing at the red area on the map. "Our next Quest lies at the edge of the Ruby Desert. It looks at least six days' travel." He glanced again at the waxing moon, frustration welling inside him. "We don't have time!" he said.

"No," Daltec said, "and I can't magic you all that far."

"Then we only have one option," said Elenna. "We need the help of a flying Beast."

Tom frowned. "I'll have to ask Ferno," he said. "But I won't let Kensa curse him too. Once we get close, we'll walk."

Tom reached for his shield and touched Ferno's glassy scale. It grew warm under his fingers. Tom sensed that Ferno was close.

Maybe he guessed we would need him, Tom thought.

Tom sent a message to the Beast.

Come. We need your help, friend. He felt the scale grow hot, then cool.

"Ferno will be here soon," Tom said. He turned to Daltec. "What magic ingredient do we need to find next?"

"Water," Daltec said.

Tom almost laughed. "Water? In the Ruby Desert?"

Daltec shrugged. "According to Aduro's research. Look…" Daltec reached into his robe and pulled out an old, worm-eaten book. Ornate gold lettering glimmered on the cover: *The Lost City of Snakes*. Daltec opened the book and turned the pages carefully. The paper was mottled and torn, and some pages were missing altogether. Finding the page he wanted, Daltec held the book

out to Tom and Elenna and pointed
to a faded passage of text.

Seeker of treasure, wander afar
Riches are found beneath the
southern star
Where the sand ends, the hot
sun bakes
Drink your fill from the mouth
of the Snake.

"I've never heard of a City of
Snakes," Tom said.

"My uncle used to tell me stories
about it," Elenna said. "But it's just a
legend. It's—"

A rush of wind whipped Elenna's
words away. Tom looked up to see
the dark, winged form of Ferno

swooping low. The massive Beast banked towards them as Tom braced himself against the wind.

Ferno lowered his great clawed feet to the ground. His wings shimmered as he folded them across his back.

Tom and Elenna raised their hands in greeting. Tom touched the red jewel at his belt.

Thank you for coming. I'm afraid we must leave at once, he told the dragon.

Ferno extended one wing to the ground, making a bridge for Tom and Elenna to climb aboard.

Storm stepped up first, followed by Silver. Tom clambered up, then turned to help Elenna onto the dragon's huge back.

"Goodbye," Daltec called, "and good luck."

Tom and Elenna waved, then held on tight.

A tremendous rush of speed pushed Tom against Ferno's scales

as the dragon swooped skyward.
Before long, the kingdom was just a
patchwork of mountains and forests,
scattered with tiny villages.

If we don't succeed, Tom realised,
*Vedra's fiery breath will destroy
those villages. I can't let that happen.*

"While there's blood in my veins,"
he muttered grimly, "we'll find that
precious water!"

MENACE IN THE WIND

"It's so desolate," Elenna said.

Wave after wave of rippling red dunes flowed past beneath them.

"Do you think this city really exists?" Tom asked.

They had been flying for half a day, and Tom had never seen a place so lifeless. There were no birds, no tracks, and not a plant in sight.

Storm was lying low, with Silver curled at his side. A scorching wind rose off the desert, filling Ferno's wings and ruffling the animals' coats. Elenna narrowed her eyes and peered ahead, her short hair blowing about her face.

"If Kensa's sent Vislak to guard water, there must be some," she said.

"Unless it's a trick," Tom said. "Kensa's as clever as she is evil." He looked down at his magic map. "According to this map, we're close."

"Tom! Look!" Elenna cried. Tom glanced up. Two swirling columns of sand were rising from the desert. As Tom watched, another giant finger of spinning sand reached into the sky, then another.

Ferno banked steeply, turning to the right. Silver growled, his paws scrabbling to hold on. Elenna lunged towards her wolf, pushing her body against his to keep him from sliding off Ferno's back.

Tom peered into the wind. The gusts were so strong, he could hardly see. Two huge twisting columns veered towards them. They started drawing together.

He touched the red jewel again, trying to steer Ferno between the winds. *Veer right!*

Ferno started to bank again, his wings dipping between the spinning towers. *We're going to make it!* Tom thought.

But as Ferno avoided the twisters,

his wing was snatched upwards. Tom
felt himself being flung sideways.
His stomach lurched as Ferno's back
dropped away beneath him. *We're
falling!* Faster and faster, they hurtled
downwards through the air. Tom felt
Ferno's panic pulsing through him.
He strained to keep his grip, but his

fingers were slipping. He glanced
down to see dunes speeding by far, far
too close. His grip gave way. The wind
rushed past him as he flew...

Oof! Tom landed on his stomach in
a bank of hot red sand. He spat out a
mouthful of grit and sat up. Nearby,
Silver was licking the dust from
Elenna's face.

Ferno was a black hump in the
distance. Tom felt a flicker of fear for
the Beast, but then the dragon lifted
his long neck and shook his head,
showering the desert with sand.

Tom scanned the dunes that
stretched away all around them.
They were the colour of old, dried
blood. There was no sign of the
sudden twisters that had brought

them down. *No sign of any living thing...*

"Storm!" Tom cried. His stallion was nowhere to be seen.

Elenna was already on her feet. "Silver, find Storm!" she said. Silver lifted his head and sniffed the air, then darted towards what looked like a tuft of dry grass. Tom felt a surge of horror. It was Storm's tail. He was buried alive in the sand!

Tom and Elenna dashed to Silver's side and dropped to their knees.

"Good boy, Silver! Good boy!" Elenna said, as they scooped away handfuls of scorching sand.

Soon, Tom could feel his horse's back, then his head.

They dug frantically until Storm's

front legs were free. The stallion clambered up from the pit, blowing sand from his nostrils. He leaned forward, and rested his velvety nose against Tom's cheek. Tom put a hand up and stroked his horse's face.

"Poor Storm!" Elenna said.

As she and Tom brushed the sand from the stallion's coat, a

huge shadow fell across them. Tom looked up to see Ferno extending his shimmering wing once more towards them, inviting them to climb back on.

Tom reached for the jewel at his belt. *There is danger ahead,* he told the dragon. *You must go back to the mountains now.*

Ferno blinked. His wing stayed where it was.

Tom didn't need his red jewel to understand. *But I've already put Ferno at risk once...*

Tom held Ferno's gaze. *You must protect your people,* he told the Beast. *Once we have completed our Quest, we will call you to bring us home.*

The dragon tossed his head, releasing a puff of fire from his nostrils. Then he moved away a short distance.

Tom and Elenna watched as Ferno lifted his magnificent wings and surged into the sky. It wasn't long before he was just a speck above the bleak horizon.

"We should leave," Tom said.

Elenna nodded. She reached into her pack and pulled out a handkerchief. "Use this to protect your face," she said.

"Good thinking," Tom said, tying the cloth about his face. Elenna did the same with another kerchief.

They looked out at the scarlet wasteland before them. *Could anyone really have lived here?* Tom wondered. He bent his shoulders into the gritty wind and struck out across the sand.

Even with the cloth in place, Tom's cheeks soon felt blasted raw. The sand beneath his feet shifted with every step.

"Let's rest," he said eventually. "We'll make better progress at night when it's cooler."

Elenna slumped into the shelter of a dune and pulled the handkerchief from her face. "I need water!" she gasped.

Tom took a flask from Storm's saddle pack and passed it to Elenna, then rummaged for the other. A horrible sinking feeling grew in the pit of his stomach as he pushed books and papers aside.

The second flask wasn't there.

"It's definitely gone?" Elenna asked, her face solemn.

Tom nodded. "We must have lost it when we crashed."

Elenna poured some water into her hand and held it out to Silver, then passed the flask to Tom. He drank a few sips and poured a little for Storm. When Tom tucked the flask away, it felt far too light. He stared out at the lifeless dunes.

Somewhere ahead lay Vislak, guarding part of the cure for Vedra's curse. And now they had an even more pressing reason to find it.

That water source had better exist, Tom thought, *or this Quest will be our last.*

ALIVE WITH EVIL

Night fell, turning the reds and
browns of the desert to inky blues
and blacks. A fat crescent moon
grinned down at Tom. He pulled
himself up to a standing position.
*Before that moon is full, I need to
have defeated three more Beasts – or
Kensa wins,* he thought. He drew a
breath of cold night air and turned
to Elenna.

"Let's go," he said. His friend was already rising from her makeshift bed, Silver at her side. She lifted her cloak from the ground and wrapped it about her shoulders.

"It's cold!" Elenna said. Storm snorted and tossed his head.

Tom scanned the bleak horizon. The sky above was prickled with stars. "The City of Snakes is south," he said, remembering the map. "If we follow the Southern Star, we can't go far wrong."

Elenna looked up at the sky and shivered. "South it is, then," she said.

They all set off into the freezing wind that howled across the desert. Tom hugged himself to keep warm, but the wind reached through his tunic like icy fingers.

"This cold is worse than the heat!" Elenna said, through gritted teeth.

"It can't be much further," Tom replied. But he didn't add what he was thinking. *If it even exists...*

They trudged on. Elenna's teeth

were chattering. Tom's eyes were gritty and his throat was sore with thirst and swallowing sand.

An enormous dune rose up before them. Storm stopped and whickered softly. Tom took his horse's reins.

"Come on, boy," he said, leading his exhausted stallion upwards. "We'll rest when we get to the top."

An icy blast hit Tom as he reached the top of the dune. He shielded his eyes and gazed out at the dark horizon. The desert was shrouded in the deep shadows of early dawn.

"Does this desert go on forever?" Elenna cried.

We must *be close,* Tom thought, staring into the greyness ahead. Then he noticed a pattern in the shadowy dunes below. Instead of endless ripples and ridges, there was a sort of spiral. It almost looked man-made.

"Elenna!" Tom cried. "Look at that!" As Tom pointed, a ray of sun broke over the horizon, flooding the desert with light. The dunes glinted, reflecting the sun, and Tom could clearly see their spiralling shape. He could see walls now, too, half-broken and buried, shining red-gold in the morning light.

"It's the city!" Elenna cried. "It has to be." She plunged over the edge of the dune towards the buried city.

Tom followed, skidding and sliding on the sand. Despite the cold and his terrible thirst, energy surged through him. *The City of Snakes is real!*

As they got closer, the shape became clearer. A high wall surrounded the sunken site. Inside were flat-roofed buildings set with small windows high up. Tom caught his breath as he looked towards the heart of the city. A mighty tower in the shape of a rearing snake rose into the sky. Weatherworn fangs glinted in its gaping mouth.

"The Mouth of the Snake," Tom muttered. "According to the legend, that's where the water should be."

"Let's hope it is," Elenna said. "I'm not sure we'll get back without it." She took their flask from Storm's pack, and shook it. It sounded very nearly empty.

There was enough for them each

to have a small drink, but then the
water was gone. And the City of
Snakes looked as dry as old bones.

Before long, they came to a gap
in the wall, flanked by a pair of tall
pillars carved with snakes. Tom held

up a hand for the others to stop, and
peered inside.

The buildings were the same dusty
red as the desert, smoothed by the
wind and broken with time. As
Tom scanned their dark windows,
he felt the hair on his arms prickle.
Someone's watching us. He drew his
sword, and led the others through
the gate.

Inside, crumbling buildings ran
either side of a half-buried road.
Elenna crossed the street and
brushed some sand from the arch
of a doorway. "Hey! Look at this!"
she said. Carvings of vines emerged
beneath her fingers. "This place must
have been beautiful once!" she said.
She pointed to a narrow, curved

channel that ran along the edge of the road. It looked like a pipe cut in half. "What do you think that is?" she asked. "They seem to run all over."

"I don't know," Tom said, distracted. He was bending to look at something by his feet. Small white bones poked through the sand. Tom uncovered them with his boot. "A snake," he said.

"And here's another," Elenna said, pointing to a pile of fragile-looking bones. "I wonder what happened."

Tom stared about the desolate street. It was so still, he could hear the sound of Elenna breathing. But something in the shadows felt alive to him. *Alive with Evil*. He lifted his sword and led the others onwards.

As Tom stepped around a corner, he spotted the toppled statue of a man. It had fallen onto its face, but it was hardly worn at all.

"What an odd statue!" Elenna said. It seemed to have been carved in a crouching position, with its hands before its face.

"It looks like it had a walking stick, too!" Tom said. There was a wooden staff lying next to the statue.

Silver sniffed at the strange carving, and started to lick its neck.

"No, Silver!" Elenna said. She started to pull her wolf away. Then she stopped. "Oh, Tom. Look!" She leaned forward and touched a tuft of matted orange hair on the statue's head. "This is real!"

Tom was at her side in an instant. What he saw made his skin crawl. The statue's face was twisted in a grimace of terror. There was a faint stirring in the sand around its mouth. *Breath!*

"He's alive!" Tom said. He started using his sword to prise away the stone. It dropped from the fallen man in hunks, until finally Tom could see patches of cloth and skin.

There was a throaty cough, and the man began to move. More stone fell away. Tom and Elenna each grabbed an arm, and lifted.

The man stood, shaking, on his unsteady feet. His face was pale under its covering of dust, his eyes wild. "A snake!" he cried. "A snake!"

"What snake? Where?" Tom said.

The man lifted a trembling finger. "Th-th-there," he stuttered.

Tom spun around. His eyes locked with the steady amber gaze of a giant snake.

Vislak!

1

THE BEAST STRIKES

Vislak uncoiled slowly, his amber eyes gazing into Tom's.

He's grown so big! Tom thought. Vislak's thick, muscled body reached halfway down the street as he glided towards them. His eyes were fierce and hungry, with none of the goodness that Tom remembered. Tom lifted his sword. He heard the creak of Elenna drawing her bow.

With a flick of his whip-like tail, Vislak turned and vanished into the darkness of a building.

He never used to be a coward! Tom thought. He followed the giant snake towards the building's door.

There was a sound behind him like a sigh of wind.

"Watch out!" Elenna cried. Tom spun around. Vislak's blunt, scarlet nose was just a footstep away. *A trick!* Tom sent the flat of his sword straight into the serpent's face.

The Beast reared up, hissing.

Tom leaped back, his sword raised. Elenna stared down her arrow and Silver crouched, ready to strike.

Vislak's tongue whipped out like a lasso and wrapped about Silver's body. Silver was jerked away through the air, growling and snapping at the shiny flesh that held him.

"No!" Elenna screamed. She let her arrow fly, but Vislak dodged with lightning speed. The arrow thudded into a wall. Tom darted forward. He leaped and sliced at Vislak's tongue, leaving a bloody gash.

Hsssss! The Beast dropped Silver and reared back from Tom's blade, his yellow-orange eyes gleaming with hate.

"Run!" Tom shouted. Storm and Silver bounded away, but the rescued stranger seemed frozen with fear.

"Come on!" Elenna cried, snatching the man's arm and pulling him down the street as Vislak surged towards them. Tom swung his sword in an arc, slashing the Beast across the nose again. The sound of Vislak's angry hissing filled the air as Tom turned and ran.

His boots skidded on sand as he dodged down a narrow alley after his friends. He heard the slither of Vislak's scales close behind him. *He's too fast!* Tom thought. *I have to slow him down.*

He sprinted for his horse and heaved himself into the saddle. He glanced over his shoulder. The Beast was almost on them, amber eyes blazing.

Tom swung Storm around so their backs were to the alley wall.

"Now kick!" Tom shouted. Storm

reared up onto his front legs. Tom
clung tight. He felt a mighty jolt as
his horse's hooves smashed into the
wall behind them. Storm turned and
leaped over the falling wall.

Tom looked behind them into the
rising dust. Blocks of stone were
crashing down across Vislak's head

and neck. As Storm's hooves hit the ground, an ear-splitting, furious hiss echoed around the city. *Vislak's trapped! But for how long?*

Tom dropped from Storm's back and dashed after Elenna and the others. They pounded down a broad street strewn with rubble, then rounded a corner into another alley. It led them onto a short road lined with tall, windowless buildings. At the end, there was nothing but a smooth, high wall. Tom stopped, and gritted his teeth. *A dead end!*

"It doesn't make sense!" Elenna said, looking up at the wall. "Why build a wall here?"

"This city's a maze," came the hoarse reply. The man they had rescued was slumped by the wall, panting. "My name is Ralph," he said. "King Hugo's Explorer. The City of Snakes was constructed so that only the folks who built it could find the temple at its heart."

Tom balled his fists in frustration. "We have to find that temple," he said. "There must be a way!"

Ralph gave a sly smile. "Well, I just so happen to have a map," he said. "Since you were kind enough to set me free, maybe I could show you..."

"Let's go then," Elenna said. "That snake could be here any second!"

Ralph's eyes glinted. "I'll take you for the small fee of half of any treasure we find."

"We didn't come here for trinkets!"

Tom snapped, glaring at him.

"Well, that's just dandy then," the traveller said, grinning. He reached into his shirt pocket, and drew out a small stack of torn, crumpled parchment.

Tom recognised it at once as pages from Daltec's book. His temper flared. "You stole that from King Hugo's library!"

Ralph blushed, then smiled again. "Let's just say I borrowed it."

"You had no right," Tom said. "Once we complete this Quest, I'll make sure King Hugo hears about this."

Ralph held up his hands. "As long as I get my treasure," he said.

Tom snatched the parchment and looked at the map. He could see that the city was spiral-shaped, with the streets forming the broken lines and dead ends of a maze. At the centre was the head of a snake. Elenna leaned over his shoulder, and tried to trace a route with her finger. She quickly reached a dead end.

Ralph dug a hand into his pocket. "You'll be wanting this," he said, tossing Tom a piece of charcoal.

Tom smoothed the map flat on the ground. He and Elenna bent over it and hurriedly traced route after route. A sudden gust of wind brought with it the rasping hiss of slithering scales from somewhere inside the city.

Vislak's got free!

Finally they found a way through. As Tom marked the map clearly with the charcoal, Ralph watched.

"So," Ralph said, "what're you two looking for, if it ain't treasure?"

"Water," Tom said, getting to his feet. Ralph stared at him open-mouthed, then laughed.

"Water!" Ralph said. "There ain't no water in the City of Snakes. This whole place is as dry as my throat. Has been for hundreds of years!"

Tom felt anger fill him as Ralph continued to chuckle. He thought of Vedra's scales gradually turning black and rounded on the explorer.

"You'd better hope there's water," Tom growled. "If there isn't, you'll be just as dead as the rest of us."

TRAPPED!

Tom squinted into the blazing sun
reflected off the buildings around
him, looking for any sign of Vislak.
The air shimmered with heat. *This
city is as hot as Uncle Henry's forge!*
Tom thought.

Elenna's eyes were on the map as
she led the way.

Ralph pulled out a rag and wiped
the sweat from his neck. "Phew!" he

said. "It's even hotter in here than the desert. It never used to be, though – it used to be a green oasis."

Tom listened carefully. Maybe Ralph knew something that would help them find water.

"People came from far and wide to bathe in the waters that flowed here," Ralph said. "But when the waters dried up, the city died. All the folks that lived here perished. Took their secrets with them. Their snake friends stayed, as legend has it, but I guess even they're gone now."

"Then where did the map come from?" Elenna asked.

"Oh, one man found his way out across the Ruby Desert," Ralph said. "He was half mad with heat and thirst, but he drew the map before he died."

"Quiet!" Tom hissed. He could hear a strange rustling sound. Soon a dry whistling also filled the air.

It grew louder as hot gusts of wind made eddies in the sand at their feet.

Tom turned around.

A whirling column of dust and debris was spinning down the street. *A twister!*

"Watch out!" Tom cried. He threw up his arms to protect his face as the wind rushed towards them.

The twister hit and Tom staggered and gasped for breath. It whirled about him, ripping at his hair and clothes. Then Tom heard a howl...

Silver! The wolf was being lifted by the wind.

Elenna screamed and swiped for Silver's paw, but she couldn't reach. Tom leaped and caught hold of Silver's leg. He braced his feet against the ground, and pulled. The wind tugged back, lifting Silver

higher. Tom looked for an escape.
There was an alleyway behind him.
He leaned back towards it, pulling
with all his strength. His feet crept
backwards as he dragged Silver out
of the wind.

Suddenly Silver fell, knocking
Tom to the ground with a thud.
They tumbled down the side street
together. Tom leaped to his feet as the
others darted into the alley behind
them. The twister whistled past.

"Are you two all right?" Elenna
asked. Her face was pale.

"Just about," Tom croaked.

Silver dipped his head and licked
Elenna's hand.

Hssssss. The papery sound cut the
air like a knife.

A snake!

Tom turned to see a small orange serpent slithering towards them.

"Hello there, little fella!" Ralph said, taking a step towards the snake. He turned to Tom and Elenna, grinning. "These little snakes are harmless," Ralph said. "They used to live here with – OW!"

Ralph jumped back, frowning. The little snake was hanging from his staff, white fangs embedded in the wood. Ralph shook the snake free, and backed away. Tom froze. He could already feel a rustling vibration in the ground beneath him. And now there was a rasping, slithering sound...and hissing.

"Tom?" Elenna said. "Tell me

that's not what I think it is." Storm paced restlessly. Tom glanced down the street. It was a dead end. He looked back the way they had come. First three, then six, then ten little snakes rounded the corner. They were quickly followed by hundreds more. Their bodies were red and brown, but their eyes were all the same...a venomous, angry yellow-orange.

They were Vislak's creatures.

A TERRIBLE BLOW

The serpents slithered forward, their tongues flickering. Hundreds of pairs of snake eyes stared up at Tom, full of hate. Their bodies twisted and writhed towards them.

"Look at their eyes," Tom said. "It's Kensa's Evil. Vislak must be controlling them."

He stepped back, and felt the wall of the dead end at his back.

"They're going to attack," Ralph cried. The small snakes were rearing up, showing their sharp white fangs.

Silver growled and leaped forward, snapping his jaws.

"No, Silver!" Elenna cried. "We mustn't hurt them. They can't help it – they're enchanted."

Silver slunk back towards the wall where Tom and the others were cornered. Storm was rolling his eyes and stamping. Ralph licked his lips nervously.

Tom's mind raced for a way out. The hideous slithering of the snakes filled his ears and their slitted eyes glowed. His head was pounding with thirst. He couldn't think! Everything seemed too bright and too loud. The

street lurched and started to spin...
Tom shook his head and blinked
hard, forcing the dizziness away.

We're trapped, he thought. *We can't
get past the snakes, so there's only
one way out.*

Tom turned to Elenna. "Over the
wall!" he said. "Take Ralph and
Silver, then run. It's the only way."

Ralph started to climb, but
Elenna hesitated.

"What will you do?" she said.
"Storm can't climb."

"So we'll have to jump," Tom said.
He put his hand on Storm's reins
and swung himself into the saddle.
Elenna frowned, but nodded. She
turned and scrambled up the wall.

Tom bent towards his horse's ear.

"You can do this," he said, "but we'll need a run-up." Storm raised his head and tossed his mane. Tom estimated the distance to the snakes, then took a deep breath. He tapped his heels against Storm's sides.

Storm surged forward, his hooves thundering over the street as they raced towards the seething mass.

Just before they reached the snakes, Tom pulled on the reins and swung Storm towards the wall. It was at least twice the height of a man.

"Yah!" he shouted, touching Storm's sides with his heels. The wind rushed past as they raced towards the wall. The closer they got, the higher it seemed, but Tom leaned low, urging Storm onwards. *We have to wait until just the right moment...*

"Now!"Tom cried. He felt Storm's muscles bunch beneath him and held tight as they soared into the air. The wall loomed towards them. It almost looked as if they would hit it! Tom braced himself...

Storm's hooves clipped the top

of the wall, then they plunged downwards and landed with a jolt in a broad, sandy street lined with high-walled buildings.

"I knew you could do it!"Tom cried, rubbing Storm's neck. But then he glanced down the dusty street and his feelings of triumph vanished completely.

Vislak's thick, muscled body was coiled right across it. Tom leaped from his saddle and drew his sword.

The Beast's broad, blunt head came up, his eyes flickering with amusement. Tom remembered the friendly creature he had met in Rion, and his anger blazed. He raised his sword.

Vislak's tongue flickered from his

mouth in a hiss of laughter. It was jet black, just like Raffkor's horn.

I have to cut it off! Tom realised. The thought of hurting his friend sent a shudder through his body. *But it's the only way to set him free.*

Tom drew himself up and charged towards the massive snake. Vislak turned and whipped his giant body around. The pointed tip of his tail flicked across the ground, whisking a swirling eddy of sand into the air. It hurtled towards Tom. *Vislak's making the twisters with his body!*

Tom threw his shield up in front of his face. The twister hit him, snatching the breath from his throat. It drove grit into his eyes and whirled about his legs, tugging him from his feet. Tom stumbled. The wind lifted him up and spun him around and around until he didn't know which way was up.

Then, just as suddenly, the wind was gone. Tom's stomach lurched as he plummeted towards the ground. He landed in a roll and scrambled to his knees, his head spinning. A shadow fell across him. He looked up, straight into the glowing, unblinking eyes of Vislak the Slithering Serpent.

The huge snake's jaws opened wide, revealing his scarlet mouth and inky tongue. Tom scrabbled to his feet and lifted his sword.

Hssssss! Vislak's black tongue flickered towards him. Tom leaped and sliced with his sword but he couldn't reach. The Beast's jaws stretched wider and wider. Tom saw two holes open in the snake's upper jaw. *He's going to spray me with venom!*

Tom lifted his shield before his face and braced his arms, waiting for the venom to strike.

"Tom!" Elenna cried from behind him. "I've come back to help!"

Tom heard an angry growl followed by the snap of teeth. He lowered his shield to see Silver's jaws clamped fast about Vislak's tail. Vislak writhed, throwing Silver from side to side. Tom dived towards the snake, just as a jet of inky venom spurted from Vislak's mouth.

"No!" Elenna screamed. The venom hit Silver, knocking him from Vislak's tail and across the street. Tom lunged at Vislak's side, but his blade fell through empty air as the snake fled towards the shadows. An arrow whistled past and glanced off Vislak's scales.

Vislak darted out of range, but

Elenna fired again and again, her face pale and her jaw clenched.

Tom dropped to Silver's side. The wolf was coated in thick, sticky goo mixed with the dust of the road. Tom tried to scrape the goo away, but it was already almost hard.

Then, with a flicker of shining scales, Silver was snatched away.

"No!" Tom cried, jumping to his feet. He leaped after his friend, but Silver and the Beast were nowhere to be seen. Tom's scalp tightened with horror. Silver had saved him from Vislak's venom. Now the Beast had taken him.

Would they ever see the brave wolf again?

THE SERPENT'S TONGUE

"Silver!" Elenna cried, darting past Tom and down the empty street.

Tom caught hold of her shoulder. "He's too fast for us to catch by running," he said, turning Elenna around to face him. Her eyes glistened with tears. "We'll have to hunt him down."

Elenna nodded, bravely blinking her tears away.

Tom checked his map. "We'll head to the temple," he said. "I'm sure we'll find Vislak there."

"If he doesn't pick us off on the way," Ralph said. The explorer was crouching against the wall. His face was pale, and he laughed nervously. "That treasure had better be something special," he added.

How can that fool still be thinking of treasure? Tom thought. Storm was gazing down the street after Silver. Tom put a hand on his horse's neck. "We'll find him, boy," Tom said. He had to believe his own words.

Tom led Elenna, Storm and Ralph through the deserted city, checking the map as he went. They travelled in silence, watching and listening for any sign of snakes, twisters or Vislak.

As they moved towards the centre of the city, the buildings became more ornate. There were fountains carved with the heads of snakes, and great open-air baths. *Once, the whole city must have been filled with the sound of water,* Tom thought. But now there was just the swish of the wind. Tom stopped. He could hear something else as well, quiet but getting louder. The hiss and slither of snakes. A lot of snakes.

"Get back!" Tom shouted. A swarm of serpents rounded the corner ahead. Ralph cowered away but Elenna stood firm at Tom's side.

"We'll face them together!" she said, notching an arrow to her bow.

Tom nodded. He turned to Ralph,
who was crouching in the shadows.
"Give me your staff!" Tom cried.
Ralph tossed his wooden staff. Tom
caught it, tied a scrap of cloth to
the end, then felt in his bag for his
flint. *Fire!* Tom thought. All animals

hate flames. The slithery hiss of the snakes filled the street. Tom glanced up. The snakes were just paces away. He struck his flint, once, twice... On the third strike, there was a shower of sparks and the cloth began to smoulder. He cupped his hands about the cloth and breathed the flame into life. Then he turned the blazing staff towards the snakes.

Elenna stayed close by Tom's side as they approached. A sea of orange eyes glared back at them. Tom jabbed his flaming staff at the creatures as Elenna fired a warning shot into their midst. They reared and hissed, their tongues angrily flickering from their mouths.

Tom stamped his feet towards the

carpet of snakes and swiped his flame at them. He could feel the red jewel in his shield pulsing with Vislak's fury.

He continued to jab and thrust while Elenna fired more shots. The snakes hissed angrily, but they started slithering away, making for the shadows. Within moments, they were gone.

Tom wiped his brow and scanned the sun-bleached street. It was empty. He dashed the blazing end of the staff against the ground, killing the flame, and tossed it back to Ralph.

Elenna swung her bow over her shoulder and looked at Tom. "Time to rescue Silver!" she said.

They hurried on, through the sweltering heat. Tom could feel Vislak's anger pulsing towards him. It beat away at him like the heat, but instead of knocking him back, it pushed him onwards. *I have to get to that temple!* Tom thought.

Vedra's life depended on it, and Silver's. And all of them needed that precious water.

They rounded a corner, and a huge tower rose up before them. Elenna gasped and Ralph whistled under his breath. The tower's sides were carved with massive scales, and its top was a mighty serpent's head.

"The temple!" Tom cried. He scanned the road ahead. Its surface was scuffed in the undulating pattern of a giant snake's track. "It looks like Vislak got there before us," Tom said, gesturing towards the trail.

"Good!" Elenna said, her hand grasping her bow. "Then Silver will be there, too."

"Remember," Tom said, "this is Kensa's Evil. We can't kill Vislak."

Elenna nodded. "But we can break Kensa's curse before anyone else gets hurt," she said.

"Storm, you stay here," Tom said. "And you, Ralph. We can't put more lives at risk."

Ralph frowned. "I'm not being left behind just when we get a sniff of that treasure," he said.

Elenna rounded on Ralph. "We aren't after your precious treasure!

We're here to save lives! But if you want to risk your life and face Vislak yourself, be our guest." She gestured towards the towering stone snake.

Ralph swallowed. He took a step back, and held up his hands. "All right," he said. "I've had my fill of venom. I'll stay here with the horse."

Tom and Elenna started forward across the temple precinct. A great fountain of carved snakes stood silent. They dashed past it and through the temple door.

Inside, it was cool and dim. Once Tom's eyes had adjusted, he found himself in a vast hall. Columns carved like snakes held up a distant ceiling. More images of snakes covered every wall and crossed the

floor. Tom scanned the shadows for any sign of a living snake.

Nothing.

Tom and Elenna crept around the temple wall, watching and listening. Something enormous, scaly and as pale as parchment lay in the shadows ahead of them. As Tom drew closer, he saw that it was the discarded skin of a giant snake.

"Vislak must have grown again!" he said. Elenna gave a muffled cry and dropped to her knees. On the floor, partly covered by the shed skin, lay Silver's lifeless body.

As Elenna started to prise the hardened venom from her wolf, Tom heard a low, laughing hiss from above.

He looked up. The Beast was coiled around a pillar high above them. His skin was now the bright red of fresh blood, and he was vast. At least twice as big as before.

Tom stared into the creature's venomous gaze and drew his sword.

Time to finish this Quest!

8

THE SERPENT ATTACKS

Tom heard the dry rasp of scales against stone and lifted his sword. Vislak was slithering slowly down the column towards him.

Suddenly the Beast's blunt nose hurtled past him. Tom slashed at it, but his blade slid off the shining scales without leaving a mark.

The giant snake drove his head into

Elenna's side, throwing her sideways
though the air. She hit the floor with
a cry. Tom darted towards her, but
the enchanted snake's muscled body
blocked his path.

Vislak's mouth opened and a stream
of thick, black liquid spurted out.
Tom leaped aside and heard the splat

of the venom hitting the ground.

From the corner of his eye, Tom
saw a flash of red. Vislak's tail was
swiping towards him. He leaped over
it, but the tail flicked again like a
giant whip.

"Aargh!" Tom's thigh exploded with
pain as the Beast's tail swept his legs

out from under him. He tumbled forward, but before he hit the ground, he felt a pressure about his waist and was plucked into the air.

Vislak's muscles squeezed his ribs. Gasping for breath, Tom lifted his sword and drove the point down into a gap between the serpent's scales.

The Beast hissed, and Tom felt

a burning pain in his chest as the coil around him tightened. Then the pressure was gone. Tom hit the ground with a terrible jolt and tumbled onto his back.

Vislak's head appeared above him. As Tom watched, the great snake's mouth opened wide.

Tom raised his shield as the venom hit with a mighty blow. Droplets like heavy lumps of clay spattered his arm. Tom rolled aside, then jumped to his feet. He could already feel his arm growing stiff as the venom hardened. He darted behind a column.

Tom glanced towards Elenna. She was sitting, clutching her side.

Splat! Another stream of venom hit the floor near Tom's feet.

Tom made a frantic dash for the next column.

Vislak darted after him, firing another blast. Tom gritted his teeth as the venom splashed the ground all around him. There was only one column left between him and the temple wall. *I'm cornered!* Tom tried to move his shield-arm, but it was stiff and useless.

I need to distract the Beast.

Tom looked about. There was a piece of stone at his feet. He picked it up, and flung it away from him as hard as he could. It hit the ground with a clatter.

Vislak's head whipped around. His body flowed towards the fallen stone.

Then Tom caught another

movement from the corner of his eye.

Ralph was tiptoeing into the temple. He looked at Tom and grinned, his whole face lit up with greed.

Tom shook his head. *Idiot! He must be after treasure. He'll get himself killed.* As Tom watched, Ralph stumbled. His staff clattered to the ground. Vislak's head snapped around and he surged towards the explorer. Ralph cowered beneath the snake, his eyes round with terror.

"Help!" Ralph cried. "Help me!"

Vislak's mouth opened wide. His great jaws stretched apart, showing his long white fangs.

Anger and frustration surged through Tom. He had to save Ralph. But could he reach him in time?

9

ALL FOR NOTHING

Tom scanned the ground for another
fallen stone, but all he could see
was sand and pebbles. *I need
something bigger!* Tom thought. He
was also worried: his shield arm was
completely dead now, just a lump of
useless stone. Then he had an idea.
He stepped back and charged at the
pillar, slamming his body against it.
The venom that held his arm smashed

and crumbled. *Yes! I can fight properly now!* Tom grabbed his shield in his right hand, and threw it as hard as he could.

It spun through the air towards the Beast's open mouth and glanced off Vislak's nearest fang, jolting his head to the side. Loose venom sprayed from his mouth, missing Ralph and splattering the temple floor.

Tom launched himself towards the snake, reaching to snatch up Ralph's fallen staff. He thrust it into Vislak's gaping mouth, jamming the serpent's jaws open.

The Beast hissed in fury, thrashing from side to side. He lifted his tail and slammed it downwards. Tom lunged and rolled to avoid the deadly blow.

Crash! The impact of Vislak's mighty tail shook the temple. Sand and chips of rock rained down from the ceiling. As Tom jumped to his

feet, Vislak lifted his tail for another vicious strike. Tom leaped aside.

Crash! More stones and mortar rained down. Vislak hissed in rage.

"I'm not going to play this game!" Tom shouted. He met Vislak's angry gaze. "It's time to set you free."

Tom dashed towards the angry snake-Beast. He leaped onto Vislak's blood-red tail, gripping the slippery scales and heaving himself along the Beast's body.

Vislak's head whipped around. His black tongue flickered past the staff in his mouth as he hissed in rage.

Tom got to his feet and ran. He skidded on Vislak's scales, but steadied himself and ran along the length of the snake's body. The Beast thrashed, trying to flick Tom free. Tom dropped to his belly and clung to Vislak's back with his arms and legs. He edged forward, hand over hand, towards the creature's massive head.

Vislak reared, sweeping Tom into the air. Tom wedged his fingertips deeper between the snake's red scales and climbed onwards. *I have to reach his tongue!*

Tom heard the twang of a bow, followed by the sigh of an arrow cutting the air. He looked down to see Elenna below him, her feet planted wide and her bow aimed at Vislak's body. The arrow glanced off the snake's scales.

Vislak started to thrash madly, jerking Tom to and fro. The temple was a blur as he clung to the writhing snake. His fingers were slippery with sweat. He couldn't hold on!

Tom swallowed hard and looked down. The temple floor was a long, long way away. *If I can't climb, I'll have to jump!*

Tom waited until a loop of Vislak's thrashing body was just below him, then he let go and landed squarely on the Beast's coiled back. Tom bent his legs and pushed off, throwing himself straight towards Vislak's jaws.

He reached out and grabbed one of the snake's sharp fangs. Vislak hissed in rage, his long black tongue whipping out past Tom and knocking the staff free.

HSSSSSsssss! The noise was tremendous. Tom pulled back his sword, and swung.

Thwack! Vislak's black tongue fell away, sliced cleanly from his mouth. Vislak's thrashing instantly stopped. The giant Beast lowered his head towards the temple floor.

Tom jumped free. He stepped around the creature's head and looked into Vislak's eyes. He touched the red jewel in his belt. *I'm sorry,* Tom told the snake, *but it was the only way.*

Vislak looked back at him, his tired gaze filled with relief. Tom laid a hand on the serpent's head and smiled. His friend was back.

Tom heard a scuffling sound, and

Ralph shot past him. "Take that!" the explorer cried.

He had grabbed his staff and held it up high, ready to strike.

Tom swung his sword at the staff, slicing it in half.

Ralph turned.

"Why did you do that?" he asked.

"Because this Beast is Good now,"

Tom told him. "The curse is lifted."

He turned and pointed to the empty space where Vislak had just been.

Ralph's jaw dropped. "Where'd he go?" the explorer asked.

"He's gone where the people need him," Tom said. "To guard a distant kingdom."

Ralph let out a long, shaky whistle. "I need to sit down," he murmured, sinking to the temple floor.

A playful growl echoed through the temple. Tom turned towards the sound, and grinned. Silver was licking Elenna's face as she pulled the last bit of stone from his fur.

"Are you both all right?" Tom asked.

Elenna nodded. "We're fine," she said, ruffling Silver's coat. "But we missed most of the action!"

Tom grinned. "We still have to find that water," he said.

Elenna jumped to her feet. "Then we'd better get started," she said.

The two of them looked around the temple. The great carved pillars that supported the roof cast shadows across the floor. In the centre of the room, four wells formed the corners of a square with a raised platform at its centre.

Tom went to look inside the first well. It plunged away into darkness. He picked up a small pebble and dropped it inside, then waited. Nothing. Not even the sound of the pebble hitting stone. He crossed to the next well. It was the same.

As dry as bone.

So was the third.

Tom felt a knot tighten around his stomach. His mouth was so dry he could hardly swallow. *Surely this can't all have been for nothing?* He crossed to the last well, and dropped a pebble.

Unwelcome thoughts flitted through his mind.

If Ralph is right, and there is no water, we will all die of thirst – and Vedra will be lost to Evil for ever.

TRUE TREASURE

The pebble made no sound.

Tom tried to control the dread and anger that raged inside him. He took a deep breath, and turned to Elenna. She was kneeling on the floor next to the platform, brushing sand from its surface. Her lips were moving as she traced some writing on the stone. Tom hurried to her side.

Elenna looked up. "Waters flow

from the hero's hand," she read. It was written on the stone next to a carved handprint. Elenna's eyes shone. "Try it, Tom!"

Tom felt a glimmer of hope. Maybe his hand would act as a key! He placed his palm over the handprint. It felt cool, and rough, and sandy – but that was all.

Elenna frowned. "I was sure that would work!" she said.

Ralph stepped out of the shadows. His face was angry and red. "There's nothing here!" he said. "Not so much as a penny. I've searched every bit of this snake's graveyard, and there's nothing but bones and sand. The treasure was a myth."

"Is that all you can think about?"

Elenna snapped. "How about helping us solve this riddle?"

"Hey!" Ralph said, pointing a finger at Elenna. "Just because we're in the City of Snakes doesn't mean you can boss me about."

Something in the explorer's words caught Tom's attention. "What do you mean 'just' because we're in the City of Snakes?" Tom asked.

Ralph smiled smugly. "Don't you two know anything?" he said. "The City of Snakes was ruled by womenfolk. The men were practically their slaves."

"How could we know, since you stole all those pages?" Tom said, but he couldn't help smiling. It all suddenly made sense. He stepped away from the plinth and looked at Elenna. "Your turn," he said.

"I suppose it's worth a try," Elenna said, her eyes sparkling.

She dropped to her knees and pressed her palm against the stone handprint.

Tom felt the ground beneath him quake. A rumbling sound started deep below the temple. Mortar and small stones skittered down the walls.

"What have you done?" Ralph said.

"What only a true hero could," Tom said. Elenna stood and backed away from the plinth. The sunken handprint was shining gold.

The rumbling sound got louder, and louder. Soon it was a deafening roar.

Suddenly, four great columns of

white, rushing water erupted from the wells. The water spouted up to the ceiling, then cascaded down again in great torrents.

"You did it, Elenna!" Tom cried. He lifted his face to the cool, fresh water and let it pour over his skin. He took great gulps of it until he was almost dizzy. Elenna stood with her hands outstretched. Ralph scooped water from the ground into his mouth, and Silver lapped thirstily.

Tom watched as the clear, bright liquid flowed along the half-pipes that crisscrossed the temple floor and out through pipes in the walls. Soon it would fill the whole city.

Tom pulled his flask from his bag. "The second ingredient of the elixir!"

he said. He filled his flask with the
flowing water, and put it back in
his bag. He touched the scale in his
shield to summon Ferno.

"We'd better get going," Tom said. "We still have two more ingredients to find."

They left the dimness of the temple and set out into the sun. Tom gasped. He could hardly believe his eyes.

"It's beautiful!" Elenna cried. Vines and climbing plants had covered the walls of the buildings and trailed across the ground. Flowers were bursting open, and every bit of dappled sunlight was crowded with basking snakes.

"This must be the true treasure the parchment spoke of," Elenna said, looking about in wonder. "The treasure of precious water. And life."

"I would have preferred gold," Ralph said, but then he smiled. "At least I ain't going to die here. For that, I thank you." He reached out and shook Tom's hand, then glanced towards Storm, who was drinking from a pipe nearby. Tom felt a rush of relief at the sight of his horse, safe and well. "It's a long way home to Avantia..." Ralph said wistfully.

"Well, you're welcome to come with us," Tom said. He nodded towards the dark, winged form of Ferno, who was swooping towards them through the sky.

Ralph's face turned from sunburned red to grey as he looked up at the fiery Beast. "On second thoughts," Ralph said, "I think I'll walk. It'll clear my head, you know?"

Tom reached towards Ralph's

breast pocket, and pulled out the
missing pages of Daltec's book. "I'll
take these," he said. "I'll return them
to their rightful place. But only once

we've saved every one of the young Beasts." Tom looked at Elenna and she smiled.

"I'm ready when you are," she said.

Tom pulled his map from his bag, and unrolled it. Deep in a patch of the Dark Jungle in Avantia's south, another name was pulsing steadily. *TIKRON*.

"It looks like we don't have a moment to lose!" Tom said.

THE END

CONGRATULATIONS, YOU HAVE COMPLETED THIS QUEST!

At the end of each chapter you were awarded a special gold coin.
The QUEST in this book was worth an amazing 11 coins.

Look at the Beast Quest totem picture on the page opposite to see how far you've come in your journey to become

MASTER OF THE BEASTS.

The more books you read, the more coins you will collect!

Do you want your own
Beast Quest Totem?
1. Cut out and collect the coin below
2. Go to the Beast Quest website
3. Download and print out your totem
4. Add your coin to the totem
www.beastquest.co.uk/totem

READ THE BOOKS, COLLECT THE COINS!
EARN COINS FOR EVERY CHAPTER YOU READ!

550+ COINS
MASTER OF
THE BEASTS

410 COINS
HERO

350 COINS
WARRIOR

230 COINS
KNIGHT

180 COINS
SQUIRE

44 COINS
PAGE

8 COINS
APPRENTICE

Don't miss the next exciting Beast Quest book in this series, TIKRON THE JUNGLE MASTER! Read on for a sneak peek...

CHAPTER ONE

RACE AGAINST TIME

The wind rushed in Tom's ears as Ferno flew onwards.

The fire dragon's great leathery wings beat slowly and steadily, bearing Tom and Elenna and their two animal companions away from the Ruby Desert.

"I'm enjoying the cool air up here," Tom said to Elenna. "Fighting snakes in a baking hot desert was hard work."

Elenna glanced back towards the rolling sand dunes. "But the giant serpent Vislak is Good again now – Kensa's power over her has gone."

Tom nodded in grim satisfaction. *That battle is over, but the war is far from won.*

Kensa the Sorceress had returned to Avantia more deadly than ever, determined to seize control of the kingdoms. She had used a terrible spell to poison the six young Beasts of Rion, stealing their goodness. Only Vedra the Green Dragon had not yet come under her thrall – but he had been infected with Kensa's lunar blood potion, like the others. At that very moment, he lay in a chamber beneath King Hugo's palace. His green scales were slowly turning to black, and by the next full moon the transformation to Evil would be complete.

All that could save him was a medicine – the Gilded Elixir – made from four ingredients scattered in the corners of the kingdom. Each was guarded by a cursed Beast of Rion intent on killing Tom and Elenna.

Tom shuddered to think what would happen if Vedra fell under Kensa's spell. *She would be almost unstoppable.*

Tom had already saved two of the Good Beasts and he had two of the elixir's ingredients in his pouch. But he knew Kensa would stop at nothing to prevent him claiming the remaining ones.

Tom glanced over his shoulder to check that his companions were all right. Storm was lying on Ferno's broad back, his legs folded up under him and the wind ruffling his mane. Silver the wolf lay at Elenna's side, his grey head in her lap, his eyes bright.

Tom unrolled the magical map. "The next Beast, Tikron the Jungle Master, will be lurking in the Dark Jungle," he said aloud.

Elenna nodded slowly. She was sitting beside him, looking at the map.

"There will be plenty of hiding places
for him there," she muttered.

Tom agreed. "We'll keep watch for
him while we search for the third
ingredient," he said. "The red root
from the hidden tree." He frowned as
he peered at the map in the growing
gloom of the evening. "But what's a

'hidden tree'? And how are we to find it in such a huge jungle?"

As Ferno flew on eastwards, night fell and ghostly clouds hung low in the sky.

"There's the Dark Jungle," Elenna said with a shudder, pointing to a wide, dark streak on the horizon.

Tom nodded grimly. *What fresh peril would be lurking in that sinister place?*

"Go down, now, Ferno," he called.

The Beast spiralled downwards and landed on the east bank of the river. Tom and Elenna and their loyal animal companions jumped down from Ferno's back. "You have to go back now," Tom said to him. "I can't risk Kensa's spell turning you bad."

Ferno narrowed his eyes, as though he didn't want to leave his friends in danger, but then he nodded his massive head. With a flurry of wingbeats, he rose into the air and began his long flight home.

As they watched him go, a point of bright blue light ignited in the air just ahead of them. The light expanded, and the wizard, Daltec, appeared, his image shimmering.

"You were right to send Ferno away," Daltec told them. "You are doing well, but time is short." He pointed into the sky. A space appeared briefly in the scudding clouds and Tom could see that the moon was almost full.

Daltec made a pass with his hand